ROMEO

JULIET

JACK

TUMULT

For Waldo and Emma

First published 1985 by
Walker Books Ltd,
184-192 Drummond Street,
London NW1 3HP

Text © 1985 David Lloyd
Illustrations © 1985 Barbara Firth

First printed 1985
Printed and bound by
L.E.G.O., Vicenza, Italy

British Library Cataloguing in Publication Data

Lloyd, David, *1945*
Waldo the tortoise. – (Great escapes)
I. Title   II. Firth, Barbara   III. Series
823´.914[J]   PZ7

ISBN 0-7445-0174-1

WALDO

THE TORTOISE

Written by DAVID LLOYD
Illustrated by BARBARA FIRTH

WALKER BOOKS
LONDON

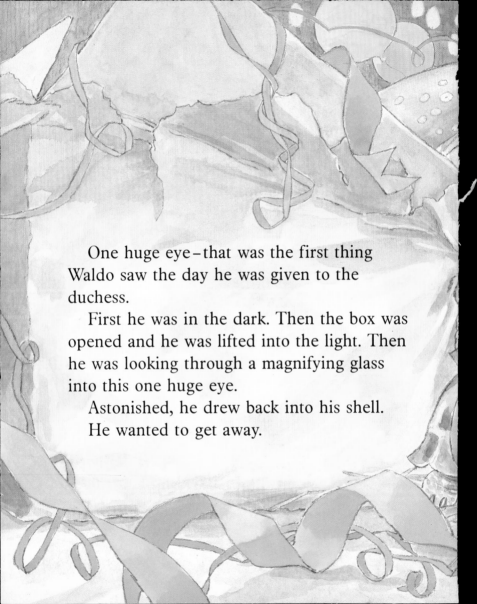

One huge eye – that was the first thing Waldo saw the day he was given to the duchess.

First he was in the dark. Then the box was opened and he was lifted into the light. Then he was looking through a magnifying glass into this one huge eye.

Astonished, he drew back into his shell.

He wanted to get away.

'Come out, funny face,'
the duchess said.
'Welcome to my party!'

Waldo liked quiet; the duchess liked noise.

Waldo like being on his own; the duchess liked parties.

The duchess changed Waldo's life–but his new life was not right for a tortoise.

When she gave lunch parties, she made him pass the salt and pepper.

When she gave tea parties, she made him pass the sugar.

When she gave fancy-dress parties, she tied
wings on him and called him Eagle; or she gave
him a crown and called him King.

The names were fine.

It was the dressing up
that was silly.

It is not easy to surprise a tortoise.

But most of the things the duchess did surprised Waldo.

When she sat in a bubble bath and read him nursery rhymes, he was surprised.

He wanted to get away.

When she tried to teach him to perch on her shoulder, he was surprised.

He wanted to get away.

When she fed him cucumber sandwiches in the garden at midnight, he was surprised.

But he ate them.

'My toothless darling!' she said.

He wanted to get away.

The duchess was wheeling Waldo
through the garden in a pram.
It was autumn, the days were
getting cold.
Waldo's eyes felt heavy.
He wanted to go to sleep.

They came to the end of the lawn, where the cannons stood.

Waldo was too tired to be surprised when the duchess put him into one of the cannons.

She thought this was a perfect place for a tortoise to spend the winter.

Now life was quiet, as a tortoise's life is meant to be. There was nothing to do but lie still and dream.

Waldo was in the dark. But in his dreams soft colours swam around him.

Through the colours other tortoises
came and went, walking slowly, talking
about their lives and dreams.

Waldo told them about the duchess,
but they only half believed him.

BANG!
The cannon fired.
The colours blew away.
Waldo hurtled up, up, up into the open sky.
The world rolled and spun.
On the lawn – now below him, now above
him – a party was going on.
The duchess was wearing pink.
'Goodness gracious!' Waldo heard her cry.
'Quickly! Quickly! Follow that cannon-ball!'

Waldo was flying, he was really flying, at last he had got away.

Goodbye, duchess!

Waldo the Funny Face looped the loop.

Goodbye, parties!

Waldo the Eagle swooped and soared.

Whoosh! Zoom! Whizz!
Flying high with the birds, Waldo the King
ruled the sky.

Then suddenly he began to fall.
He couldn't stop falling.
The earth came closer and closer.
The sky grew dark.
There was just a little patch of pink in
one corner of the sky, like a handkerchief
floating down.
With the last of his strength, Waldo swung
towards it.

The handkerchief turned out
to be a parachute. When Waldo
hit it, it swallowed him softly,
then lifted him up again, cushioning his fall.

He was safe, unhurt, resting on the
parachute.

There was a hole in the middle of it.

He went carefully to the edge of the hole
and looked down.

No! No! How could this be?
The duchess dangled below.

They reached the ground.

The duchess landed badly, losing her helmet and her magnifying glass.

Waldo landed softly as the parachute billowed down.

'Oh dear! Oh dear!' said the duchess. 'I've lost my helmet!'

She saw Waldo, but not very clearly.

'My helmet,' she said.

She picked him up and banged him hard
on her head, trying to put him on.
Waldo and the duchess fell down.

Waldo was on his back.

The world was upside down.

Upside down, he saw the duchess stand up and wander away, pulling the parachute behind her. She did not see him.

He lay and rocked and kicked his legs – but it was no good.

He was hopelessly, helplessly stuck.

He might have stayed there for ever had Jack not found him and turned him over.

Dear Jack – the cleverest dog in the world!

There are seven animals in the gang today.
They have all had great escapes.
They live together and travel together.
They are friends.
Tonight they are in the heart of a city, and
it is Waldo's turn to tell the story.
He half believes it is true.

'One huge eye – that's what I saw when
I first met the duchess,' he begins.
And the story which he tells is the story
you just heard.

WALDO   LADY LOUDLY   MOT